The Moon Visits Paradise

II

Benedicta Ibidunni

Table of Contents

First published in the UK in 2023 by Benedicta
Ibidunni

ISBN 978-I-7395758-I-6

Copyright ©Benedicta Ibidunni 2023

Illustrations © Benedicta Ibidunni

Chapter I

Osupa Moon Island

Osupa island, otherwise known as Moon Island, is a tropical paradise between the northwest Atlantic Ocean, off the coast of Africa. The original settlers named their home Osupa because the sun is seen setting, as the moon rises simultaneously. Watching this phenomenon gives a transcendent feeling, of being on another planet entirely. It is said the moon visits paradise for a moment each time it rises in the east, and the sun sets in the west.

The island of Osupa has a vast green mountainous region, flanked by smaller island islets. It has a tropical rain forest with breath taking waterfalls, and bright coloured tropical plants, and birds. The lakes and rivers twist and bend in different directions throughout the island. It is home to a vibrant and colourful coral reef teeming with marine life of every description, protected by steep rock cliffs, forming a natural defensive barrier along the coastline. The cliffs restrict access to large vessels entering Osupa harbour.

There were three fortresses on the island, which gave soldiers an arial view of the waters beyond. The colour of the ocean is so clear, it mirrors the clear sky above. Boats dock in the harbour to transport goods and passengers. Beyond the harbour there is a huge marketplace with traders, bars, and food stalls of every kind. From the dock, an array of whitewashed buildings, with terracotta roofs of every shape and size, is built into the leafy hillside above.

The people of Osupa originate from the Yoruba kingdoms in the western region of Africa. Different ethnic groups have settled on the island over centuries. Some settlers were survivors of shipwrecks seeking refuge from war torn regions. Islanders believed in the goddess of the oceans and rivers, who protects them, and provides good health and new life. The ocean provides fishing, farming, and safe passage for their vessels. In return islanders respect and protect the ocean and rivers.

The island is known as a wealthy trading port. A place where people come from all over Africa to trade goods. The history of the Osupa kingdom can be traced back to 3150 BC. It was a place battles were fought against invading armies over millennia. On the island, power is shared between the monarchy and advisers representing the people. When the monarch dies, power passes to the next ruling house. In the seventeenth century the island closed its territorial borders, to protect against pirate ships, sailing through the west coast of Africa. Merchant ships were vulnerable to raids and the seizure of their cargo. If captured the crew could join the pirates, face death or enslavement. To protect the island, they closed their borders from the 17th century, until the raids ceased, and the region settled.

The closure of the island stopped the threat of pirate raids, merchants trading in drugs and alcohol and missionaries teaching foreign religions. Doctors and scientist were welcomed on the island to complement their teachings and the advancement of Osupa civilisation. The border closure allowed them to thrive and developed peacefully, uninterrupted by the outside world for centuries. The Islanders were a race of scholars, artists, and warriors. They had a sophisticated civilisation hidden from the outside world for centuries. Their teachings were passed down in pictographic scrolls, tablets and stories passed from one generation to the next. Their language was both verbal and nonverbal. They had a rich artistic culture of talking drums, music, dance, and artistry. One of their traditions was to mark their upper arms with the symbol of Osupa.

The island was known as a place of refuge and trade, where settlers could build a life for themselves and their families. Centuries later the decision of the ruling Queen had a profound and positive impact on the survival of the kingdom.

At the end of the boarder closure new allies were formed with five of the most powerful kingdoms on the continent. This secured power and stability for Osupa, which gave her military neutrality as an important trading port. The island was able to develop a thriving and extremely successful industry, producing the rarest of black pearls and gold. The ecosystem on the island created the perfect environment for cultivating black lipped Oysters, which produce unique black pearls. The island had huge deposits of gold in underground caves, which created high quality pure gold. The island became well known, as a centre for superior quality pearls and gold.

The gold and pearl industry created wealth, for the Osupa monarchy and the islanders. The prominent gold and pearl industry brought traders, visitors, and settlers to the island from different parts of the African continent.

History of invaders

Osupa island was targeted by different invaders throughout their history. Their armies were known as formidable warriors. The battle cry of the Osupa armies approaching instilled fear in their enemies. Their fighting techniques in combat were well renowned because of the small number of casualties. Training for combat started from childhood to protect themselves and their kingdom when the time came. Their fighting skills became second nature from a young age, which created peace and mutual respect. The fighting technics taught their fighters to think two steps ahead of their next strike.

History had taught the kingdom of Osupa, to prepare for the possibility of war in times of peace. Their ancestors' writings warned of a dark time in history, when Osupa was invaded by the sun kingdom. The invasion started with the landing of foreign emissaries, who asked for an audience with the Queen. The emissaries claimed they came in peace to create a trade treaty.

They brought strange and magnificent gifts with them for the Queen. They were granted permission to set camp on the island, under the protection of the Queen for two weeks. Osupa secret agents were deployed to monitor the activities of the emissaries as a precaution. The emissaries had concealed their real mission on the island. They were military scouts, conducting an operation to catalogue the population, terrain, and military capability of the kingdom. Their objective was to invade the island, capture the occupants and kill as many islanders as they could. Two weeks after the scouts arrived, war ships from the Sun kingdom, were spotted in their territorial waters, on the high seas from the watch towers around the island.

The sun kingdom had planned to use the element of surprise. A week after the Sun scouts arrived on the island. Osupa military agents discovered their plans of invasion. The army acted quickly by evacuating families living in coastal settlements around the huge island, in preparation of the invasion. The scouts from the Sun kingdom staying on the island were captured. Interrogators were able to extract vital information about the invasion plans.

On the night of the invasion, enemy boats approaching Osupa harbour were greeted by archers shooting burning arrows and flammable oil into enemy ships. The attempted invasion by the sun kingdom was unsuccessful. The armies underestimated the capability and military intelligence of the Osupa army. Sun soldiers were cut down before they had a chance to reach the island.

The attempted invasion reminded the Osupa kingdom that the island was vast and vulnerable in some regions. They tightened their defences and ensured the island was protected and impenetrable.

Chapter 2

Jibola Daughter of Osupa

Osupa was an island steeped in mystery and legend. It was said that some islanders were born with the gift of prophecy. Jibola was one of those children. She was extraordinarily intuitive, even as a young child. She had a natural gift for reading people and situations. Her instincts were perfect compared to the adults around her. Her abilities meant she knew instinctively if she was lied to. For Jibola reading people was like reading code.

She could sense dangerous situations before they happened. Jibola had made exact predictions despite contrary information. Her ability to predict started as a child and got stronger the older she became. She could tell important events were about to happened days before they occurred. When she was a young child, she told her father he would have an accident days before it occurred. Her warnings and dreams about the accident helped to save her father's life. Her ability to predict was strongest when she was near the incident or person involved.

Jibola was removed from the loving care of her parents, and recruited into the intelligence academy when a teacher from her school informed the authorities of her gift. Once she was able to control and harnessed her abilities, she was recruited into the intelligence service in charge of the kingdom's security. Jibola was young but they wanted her to start her training early. She was told she was destined for greater things, but she did not want greater things, she just wanted to remain with her family. Sadly, that option was taken away from her.

Her intuition helped her in combat because she knew her opponent's next two or three moves. Jibola became increasingly confident and excelled in training. Her intuition allowed her to read people and anticipate their behaviour. Her gift gave her an advantage in decision making, but it won her some enemies.

At the academy Jibola found out her gift made her a target. She was younger than most of the recruits. Her mother had objected about the recruitment, but she was assured it was like a boarding school for talented young people. Once the other recruits found out about her abilities, she felt isolated and ostracized by some of them. Most of the younger recruits admired her skills and nicknamed her Ekun(tiger). All the younger students were close. They bounded and tried to protect each other from the bullies.

One group of older recruits took a dislike to Jibola. She was called names and told she was flaunting her abilities when she did well in class. Most of these recruits were older than Jibola and had waited for years to get into the academy. They felt it was unfair to recruit someone so young, that excelled where others with more experience had failed.

Jibola was bullied and picked on in class, and socially after training. She was an excellent fighter, therefore picking a fight with her was unwise. The only way to try and break her moral was to taunt her. One of the trainers noticed the bulling a few times and realised

Jibola was being bullied because she was younger and talented. The bullying was starting to affect her emotionally. She did not want to leave her room after class or socialise with the other trainees.

One of her trainers noticed a dramatic change in her demeaner and self-esteem. She decided to investigate what was causing her change in behaviour. Once she found out what was happening, she made sure the bullies were dealt with accordingly. The trainer's quick action meant Jibola could complete her training and regain her confidence.

Once Jibola left the academy she rose through the ranks quickly to become a high-ranking diplomat representing Osupa. Her mission was to represent the kingdoms interest abroad and promote the relationship between Osupa and Ajee. A large part of her role was to negotiate trade agreements between kingdoms. Osupa had a long-standing trade relationship with Ajee as both kingdoms had great power and wealth. Jibola travelled often visiting different kingdoms on the west and northern coast of Africa, on diplomatic missions on the behalf of the kingdom. When she travelled her personal staff included her personal guards, sworn to protect her. Her duties sometimes meant she was placed in dangerous or compromising positions. She had worked for many years as an accomplished spy for the kingdom. She had uncovered conspiracies against the kingdom from other territories. She had conducted counterintelligence operations against enemy spies trying to infiltrate her kingdom. She wanted a change. She welcomed her new role as a diplomat, which required a different set of skills.

Jibola was returning to the kingdom of Ajee on a visit. She was invited to a grand banquet at the home of her friend Amardi. She enjoyed his banquets, because it created an opportunity to meet interesting people in business and the pollical arena. Amardi had told her to prepare for an interesting exhibition at the end of the banquet.

The Banquet

Amardi, was a wealthy entrepreneur in Ajee, with social and political connections internationally. He often had lavish banquets on his private estate. His events never disappointed. Jibola had been looking forward to the banquet since she received the invitation. She could see the bright lights and festivities in the distance as she arrived with her entourage. Hosts and entertainers welcomed her. There were fire eaters, dancing contortionists, musicians and the lively chatter of friends embracing and greeting each other. The guests were dressed in opulent, colourful attire. Musicians played in the great hall with the hum of voices and laughter in the great hall. Jibola loved Ajee music. There was a lady singing an emotional love song. The sound of her silky voice filled the hall and commanded everyone's attention. She was dressed in a beautiful caftan, with patterned embroidery symbolising her status. She had a backing orchestra of djembe drummers and kora players.

Jibola started looking for Amardi and wondered why he was missing the performance. Amardi saw her first across the great hall and walked across to greet her with a warm embrace. He was pleased to see his friend. He wanted to tell her; all she had missed while she was away on her travels. Jibola was happy to see him too.

She had missed his grand parties, and his humour. He was someone she trusted and respected.

Amardi opened the huge banquet and his guests taking their seats. There was food and wine of every description and an array of interesting fruits, she had never seen. The highlight of the evening at the end of the meal, was an exhilarating display, of what sounded and looked like an illusion of thunder and lightning. It made a sound that vibrated straight through their bodies. The loud noise was, followed by objects propelled into the air, which turned into colourful flashes of lighting in the night sky. It created an amazing display. Jibola was impressed and determined to understand exactly what the Black power was composed of and why it was so powerful.

Amardi presented her with three gifts after the display. The first gift was a large box filled with the finest African coffee beans from Ajee. The second gift was a large jar filled with the finest honey from the tropical mountains. The last gift was a heavy box filled, with what looked like coarse black sand. He explained, the black powder, in the box created the incredible display they saw. He knew

Jibola would be excited when she saw it. He explained it was known as black powder from far east Asia. A newly discovered invention used for entertainment at parties and celebrations.

Amardi showed Jibola a small demonstration of how to prepare the powder. He explained it was highly flammable and could be fatal if used incorrectly. He said, storage rooms of black powder had exploded when used or stored incorrectly. He knew a man that had lost both his legs in such an explosion. Jibola assured him it would be stored safety. She was keen to understand exactly how it worked. She wondered what it was made from, and why it was so powerful.

Amardi admired Jibola. She held a highly coveted position in government, which commanded a great deal of influence and respect. She was a shrewd woman. She had no tolerance for arrogance or lies. She was cautious when dealing with people and had tight inner circle of friends. Jibola was drawn to kind and compassionate people because of the trauma she experienced as a young woman.

There was a mutual attraction between Amardi and Jibola. He enjoyed giving her extravagant gifts, and she always had gifts for him from her travels. They enjoyed spending time together and started developing a romantic relationship. Despite her commitments and travels on diplomatic missions. Jibola completely dedicate her life to serving the kingdom of Osupa. Her unwavering loyalty and commitment to her responsibilities as a diplomat left no room for love or a romantic relationship. Jibola met Amardi on one of her missions. Since their first meeting the great wall she so carefully built around her heart had started to disintegrate piece by piece.

Amardi is an adventurer and an affluent merchant. He started falling in love with Jibola from the moment they met. He admired her strength, and loyalty to her kingdom, but he had no intension of allowing it to prevent the development of their relationship. She had a strength of strength of character matched only by her striking beauty. Amardi wanted them to share an adventure of travelling to new places unfamiliar to Jibola together. He knew the perfect retreat where they could stay and completely relax. They would want for nothing, and all their needs would be catered to.

Amardi and Jibola's Voyage

Amardi convinced Jibola to take a voyage with him around the coast of African visiting different cities, cultures, and incredible landscapes. Their voyage would eventually arrive at a hidden location. They travelled through the tropics to reach the great waterfall, where the earth divided a great river, to form a powerful, thundering waterfall several hundred feet deep. The power of the waters crashing into the earth below created a vision of steam rising into the clouds above.

On their journey they visited the ancient city of Ife. The capital and religious centre of the Yoruba people and considered a holy city. Jibola's ancestry was from Ife. She had wanted to visit the city for many years, but the opportunity had never presented itself.

Amardi had businesses in Ife trading in gold, copper, leather, and spices. Jibola felt drawn to the area and saw so many things that felt familiar from her family's history.

While in Ife Jibola met Ardo, Amardi's friend, who invited them to his home for dinner. He lived in the heart of the old city. His house was surrounded by a high wall. In his grounds he had a magnificent garden. Jibola noticed the meticulous way the garden was kept and nurtured. If was uncommon to own such a treasure in the city. Jibola walked round the garden admiring the bright flowers and orange trees. Amardi sat in the garden drinking cold juice and watching Jibola as she walked looked at different flowers. A few after their arrival two men arrived carrying large trays of food emerged from the house that looked. The food looked and smelt delicious. Ardo was joined by his wife, Zahra and their two young children. They spent the rest of the afternoon eating and talking, as the children played in the garden.

After spending the afternoon with Ardo and his family, they thanked them for their hospitality and set off for Amardi's home.

They arrived at his home in the evening. They were greeted by Jolloh, who looked after the house while Amardi was away on his travels, trading. The courtyard at the front of the house was the first thing Jibola noticed when they arrived. It was truly impressive. It was designed in white and blue mosaic. There were three arched entrances into the house. Jibola admired the architecture of the building.

She could see Amardi had poured their heart into creating the perfect home. She could hear the gentle sound of water trickling out of the fountain at the centre of the courtyard. The entrance felt welcoming. Jolloh had prepared an evening meal for them both. He knew Amardi was arriving that evening. He had made them jollof rice with lamb stew. There was a bowl of fruits, dates, and a jug of water in the centre of their dining table.

Jibola was exhausted after spending all day enjoying the garden and running around with Ardo's adorable children.

The next day they started their voyage to the hidden location. It took them a few days to arrive at their destination. They travelled by land with a group of helpers to the waterfall. Jibola was in awe of what she saw. The sheer depth of the waterfall below, was an unbelievable sight. She felt drawn to the edge of the falls. She could not resist looking down. Every cell in her body was thrilled by the sound of the thundering waterfall. She looked at Amardi with loving eyes and said,

"Thank you for bringing me to your special place. It's incredible. You travel to all these amazing places, meeting new people. You are constantly on the move, yet you have so much energy. You are always energised making everyone feel special."

He held her close and gave her a kiss that seemed to last an eternity. Amardi said,

"Now you know where my energy comes from! I wanted you to see this place. It is humbling and a reminder, you only have one life. You owe it to yourself to enjoy each day. You and I are so small and insignificant compared to this stunning creation. While we are here, we will rest, we will swim in the river below. We will eat, make love and most importantly we will heal our minds and bodies. Everything is arranged and prepared for us. "

They stay in a stone cabin near the falls for a few days, S before heading back to Osupa. Jibola and Amardi had a son, who became a great states man in Ajee. Her discovery of gun powder meant the kingdom of Osupa could defend itself for key periods throughout history. She realised gun powder provided the protection the island needed. The Kingdon was for ever indebted to her for her dedicated service to her kingdom. Jibola continued to serve Osupa as a diplomat for many more years to come.

She went missing, presumed killed on a mission visiting a foreign territory when a military uprising erupted. Jibola was caught in a skirmish on her way her was to a conference. Her legacy lives on in Osupa today, as the diplomat that discovered the islands most powerful defence weapon. The discovery changed the history and security of Osupa for centuries to come. Her gift of prediction was inherited from the female line in her family. There had been other women in her family that were born with a similar gift but none as powerful as Jibola.

Chapter 3

Ife Mi - My Love

In present day Osupa there is a grand wedding. There are photographers recording videos, and guests are taking pictures on their phones. Celebrations and music fill the magnificent mosaic courtyard, shaded by palm trees. The open roof and grand fountain in the centre create a perfect oasis. The sound of talking drums, announcing the wedding of Simi and Dami, could be heard in the hills beyond as guests danced to celebrate Simi and Dami's wedding.

The families of the bride and groom were dressed in all their traditional outsits, with red coral and gold necklaces. There was a spectacular array of beautifully dressed guests, in traditional attires with gold Gele head wraps. The children giggled and played, as their mother's tried and failed to stop them running around the courtyard. The gathering looked like a magnificent royal wedding in all its splendour.

Dami's family presented the dowry to Simi's extended family. The dowry was filled with bales of fabric, jewellery, gifts, and money. They had come to receive the new bride. The ceremony was to ask Simi's parents, for her hand in marriage.

It was a happy day filled with Yoruba ceremonial traditions. There was a grand feast laid out for the guests. A dancing procession of women, moved in step, to the rhythm of talking drums. Family and friends joined the train of dancers to the centre of the courtyard. The musicians played their talking drums, and beaded Sekere calabashes to the sound of women singing love songs. The guests were seated in the courtyard, where the families assembled, to celebrate the symbolic passage of Simi leaving her family as a single woman, to join her husband's family as his new bride.

The funniest part of the ceremony is when Dami identifies Simi under a woven veil, out of all the lovely, veiled woman presented to him. Each women presented is a sister, a cousin, or a friend.

Each woman is dressed in their traditional bridal clothes, making the selection more difficult. Dami is asked by Simi's aunt,

"Dami, we are gathered here because we understand you have come to ask for one of our beautiful daughters. We have many gorgeous women in our family, which one are you enquiring about."

You could hear the chatter from the families and friends gathered. Every so often you can hear suppressed laughter and giggles.

Dami said, "I am asking for the brightest and most magnificent star in your family."

The crowd is happy with his response.

Simi's aunt said, "Dami, you have to select the magnificent star you chosen, because all our stars are magnificent."

Each woman came out dressed as a traditional bride. Dami rejected six veiled women without lifting their veils, and each time he was asked if, he was sure.

Simi's aunty said, "Dami, are you sure! you have not seen the magnificent star you are looking for, because you have rejected six beautiful women."

He said, he was sure. The seventh time, it was Simi, and he lifted her veil to the delight and cheers of everyone. Simi looked gorgeous, in her orange and gold Aso Oke bridal attire. She had coral beads round her neck, and long braided hair and an elaborate gold coloured Gele head wrap. Her nails were painted, and her hair looked immaculate. Simi's hands and feet were covered in henna patterns, designed by her friend Halima.

Dami had chosen correctly. The consequences of choosing the wrong bride would have been embarrassment for Dami, followed by teasing and laughter from Simi's family. All in keeping with the ceremonial festivities of the special day.

Once Dami and Simi were united, both parents placed their hands on them and prayed for their happiness, enduring love, respect, and patience,

Simi's mum, Yemisi became emotional and tearful at the end of the ceremony. She looked at her daughter and remembered their special moments together. When they were together there was always mischief, warmth, and laughter. Yemisi knew she would miss Simi at home. The family home would not be the same without her around.

Simi knew just what to say, when she was worried or unhappy. Simi had a positive attitude to life. She liked experiencing new adventures and new opportunities. She was fiercely protective of those she loved and cared about. Yemisi was proud of her. She had achieved what she wanted by embracing all life had to offer.

Simi's dad, Timi could see his wife was getting emotional. He gave her a warm hug and a kiss. He reminded her Simi would come round to spend time with them and her younger siblings. Drummers, dressed in traditional kaftan like agbada, played talking drums, and sang love songs about their journey together.

Yemisi invited her friend Sade and her husband Luke, to the wedding. Sade had become a good friend of Yemisi and one of her best customers. Sade had referred several interior designers to Yemisi's ceramic pottery business, which contributed to the expansion of her business. Yemisi was now making huge pots for the international market. The quantities ordered had increased dramatically. Sade's support had made a big impact.

Sade had bought many traditional terracotta pots from Yemisi. Her family were one of the oldest custodians of Osupa heritage, and the ancient art of pot making. Yemisi had taught Simi from a young age, the skill of moulding clay, making pottery, and using a kiln. This was the same way her grandmother had instructed her, and her mother before her. Simi had learnt to build a kiln from dried wood and branches.

Sade liked the unique style of pottery especially Yemisi made, with traditional patterns, and pictographic inscriptions. Yemisi had a small team of pottery makers in her workshop. The pottery they made was of the finest quality Sade had seen. They put a great deal of effort into their creations. Sade enjoyed sitting with Yemisi in her workshop when she visited. They would talk about life in Osupa and her new creations for hours.

Sade had watched Simi, grow into a bright young woman. She the years had passed quickly, and now she was getting married. Sade was happy for Simi and Dami. Simi had big dreams and expectations for the future. She was ambitious and determined, as were all the women in her family. She was a descendant of the royal house of Osupa. She was taught to dream big and fight for what she wanted in life. Simi fought to get into the fine Arts college, and never looked back. There were a few bumps along the way, but she persevered.

She developed her craft and worked tirelessly. She spent long hours creating one off pieces. Her positive attitude gave her the desired outcome. Simi decided early on, to sell her ceramic designs to help with her tuition. She had a gift for making unique pieces. Fortunately, there was constant demand for her work online shop and through social media. She had a blog where she spoke about her artwork.

Chapter 4

Dami and Simi's journey

Simi and Dami had known each other since childhood because their mothers were close friends.

Dami, had loved Simi for as long as he could remember. The grand plan he had rehearsed in his mind a hundred times over, was to ask Simi to marry him once he secured a decent property and the new job he applied for. He was still living at home with his Mum and Dad. That needed to change. He was determined to secure a place they could call home before he proposed. Their relationship had grown in the last few years. Simi was his soul mate. He loved her strength and her warmth.

He missed her when she was away, and she always made him feel special. She had a way of making him feel like the most important person in the world. He looked forward to raising a family with her, as far as he was concerned Simi was his future. He had never had those feelings for any other woman. He knew he wanted to grow old with Simi. He found a great property with plenty of space and a large garden. He knew Simi would love the garden because she loved nature and open spaces. He had saved enough for the wedding and was offered the job hr applied for.

On their evening walk by the stone lake, Simi told Dami, she would be spending more time in the city for her business and the art exhibitions. There was constant demand for her work, and most of her clients were based off the island. Logistically it was easier. Dami admired Simi's entrepreneurial spirit and drive. He did not know anyone else, that young who had a business.

The Farm

Dami travelled to Faversham, Kent, in the UK for a year, to work as an agriculturalist on a fruit farm. He was ambitious and had great plans for his future as a farmer. He wanted to experience different farming methods in a new climate, with extreme seasonal changes. He was given the opportunity to live and work on the fruit farm in Faversham. He was looking forward to autumn and summer. He arrived in autumn, when the evenings were longer, the days shorter, but the air was a little colder. The grass of the forest behind the farm, was covered in red and orange leaves. The forest had tall red maple trees. Their branches formed a canopy above of red and orange leaves above. Dami listened to the leaves crunching beneath his boots as he walked along the path watching the sun disappear behind the trees. He felt the chill in the air even with his heavy coat and boots. He was amazed by the difference in climate. The trees and plants at home, were green and lush all year round apart from the dry harmattan season, when the grass dried forming a golden-brown colour.

The chilly air felt dry, unlike the humid light air he was used to. His could not understand why his skin was so dry. It was something he had not experienced before. Dami stayed in touch with Simi while he was on the farm. They spoke daily about the farm life, and the new people he had met, especially the locals and the pubs. He talked about the difference in cultures, and how welcoming and friendly people were when he went into town. Most of the time they spoke about how much they missed each other, and what they wanted to do to each other when he returned home. Simi sent him videos and pictures of life in Osupa.

Simi had experienced living in a city as a student for a few years. She exhibited her work in galleries and made income from the pieces she sold. She did not mind living in the city for short periods, but Osupa was where her heart was. City life was not as fulfilling as she had hoped.

Simi found herself missing life on the island. The holidays breaks at home were never long enough. Leaving her family and Dami for long periods was always a struggle. When she took friends to the island from the city, they thought she was crazy to even consider living in the city. Osupa was truly a paradise; most people never experience living in such an idyllic place. The ocean, the bustling harbour, the ancient architecture, and the ruins made it a unique historical place to call home.

Dami and Simi spent their time on the Island swimming, visiting the small islets close to the island. In the evenings they would build a fire on the beach and snuggle up, watching the stars in the night sky. Dami had a boat, they used for snorkelling in the coral reef. Thinking about Simi gave him something to look forward to when he got home.

Everything came alive in summer. The fields were covered in plants and flowers of every kind. Dami came across a fearless fox in the woods a few times on his walks. In Summer he realised how much people loved their dogs. He saw dogs of all shapes and sizes, there were so many. It felt as though everyone had a dog, apart from him and he wanted one desperately. On the farm they had two handsome Boxers, he sometimes took on walks in the woods. He enjoyed his time in Faversham and was happy to be going back to Osupa.

Planning the Wedding

When he returned home, he felt like a changed man. Everything looked and felt different. He was starting a new job with a tropical fruits company. Simi was home when he arrived. He had missed her, and could not wait to see her smile, and the way her eyes lit up when she saw him. They were both ecstatic when they saw each other. He hugged her and did not want to let go.

Dami planned to ask Simi's father, for her hand in marriage according to tradition. Once he got her father's blessing, he planned to ask Simi. He wanted to do it the traditional way, because he respected her father and knew he was an old-fashioned man. Her father gave his blessing because he liked Dami. Simi's father understand Dami loved and respected his daughter a great deal. He knew Dami was kind, thoughtful. He had seen him grow up into a young man he would be proud to call his son in-law. That was enough for him.

Simi's father and Dami had their own relationship. They had spoken several times, when Dami was at their home. He wanted to know what Dami wanted for his future. He had seen how passionate he was, about owning his own farm. It had not gone unnoticed, that Dami was hard working and always planning for the next big venture for the future. Both men had a love of football. They would talk and joke for hours about their teams' successes and disappointments.

Dami's mother knew they loved each other, which made her happy about their union. Simi was in love with Dami. He was her soul mate and the love of her life. In the last few years, their relationship had blossomed. Simi had a feeling he was going to ask her to marry him.

They had spoken about their future many times, especially during their video calls, while he was in Faversham. Simi knew she wanted to spend her life with him. He wanted Simi to know he was committed and invested in their relationship for the future. He had been incredibly anxious all day about asking her to marry him. He had not slept the night before his adrenalin levels were so high.

"You know you can tell me anything, right?"

When they arrived at the centre of the of the stone bridge, above their favourite lake. Simi was Dami said, "I have an important question I want to ask you. Will you do me the greatest honour of becoming my wife."

Simi was delighted. She looked into his eyes, with a huge smile said, "Yes, I love Dami, yes you are my best friend, and yes, I will marry you."

Dami picked her up by the waist and swung her round in his embrace. He kissed her slowly on the lips.

Dami said," You have made me the happiest man on the island. If you see someone walking on air that will be me."

Chapter 5

Sade's gift

Sade looked forward to her long walks along the shoreline. She liked looking at the ruins of the ancient towers on the cliffs of Osupa. It ruins reminded her of the island's rich history and her ancestry. Sade had inherited the gift of sight and prediction. When she was younger her abilities came to her naturally. Her mother helped her to understand how to take control. She taught her to be careful and responsible with her abilities. She was told it was best to keep her predictions to herself. Sade knew the only person she could tell was her mother. Her mother's priority was to protect her from becoming targeted because of her gift.

Sade realised early on that her predictions made her a target. Her abilities made those people around her uncomfortable and sometimes frightened. Her predictions were powerful, but she learnt to lock them away deep down. She never spoke about what she knew or what was coming. The only person she spoke to about her dreams and predictions was her mother.

Sade walked to the old fortress along the cliffs of the island. She could smell the vast expanse of the ocean as she approached the edge. She enjoyed standing on the tower, watching the rhythm of the waves as they crashed against rocks below. The ocean made her feel calm and completely at peace.

Sade has a successful architectural construction company in the city. It is well known for innovative and contemporary design. She started her business in landscape architecture, creating stunning outdoor spaces for large private residential homes and corporate properties. Her designs grace the pages of popular architectural magazines featuring innovative, sustainable design. She had won design accolades for the last ten years. Her creations stood out, and her company is one of the most dominant in the industry.

She had spent several years working for design architecture companies, unfortunately her commitment went unrewarded. She felt disillusioned and unfulfilled. She decided to create her own design company. She started with a small investment and client base, which developed into a successful company. Her sleepless nights, and perseverance paid off. She started seeing returns on her investments.

Sade liked relaxing at home after a long day. Her home was ocean facing, on the outskirts of the city. It took a little longer to get home in the evening, but it was worth the drive. She looked forward to a relaxing weekend. That evening, she showered and had a light meal before she went upstairs to her studio.

Her studio was where she had the freedom to create uninterrupted. She nodded her head gently to the sound of smooth jazz, as she sketched on her pad. Sade had a tall glass of her juice, perched within reaching distance. Her phones were on silent, no calls, no interruptions only music, cascading round the studio. She was in her creative zone; nothing could penetrate her mood. She kept drawing, until she realised it was late. She dragged herself to bed completely exhausted.

The next morning, she woke up early, just as the sun started rising to bird songs. She opened the French windows in her bedroom onto the balcony, covered in scented jasmine climbers. She could see the red African tulip trees at the back of the garden. Sade stood staring at the red blooms on the trees, when she felt the warm embrace of his strong, warm arms gently pulling her towards him. It was Luke. She smiled as she turned round slowly in his embrace, placing her arms around his shoulders with a kiss.

Sade said, "Morning, my love, did you sleep well."

Luke said, "Yes darling and you?"

Sade said, "Goodness that coffee looks and smells perfect. When did you get up."

She looked into his eyes, as he handed her a cup of coffee. His eyes still had the ability to make her heart melt. She thought how caring, and considerate he was. He still knew how to make her feel special. Luke is tall and handsome, with an athletic build. Sade still remembers the day they got married with all their friends, and family to witness their special day. His charism draw attention when he entered a room. Her favourite quality about Luke, is his ability to put a smile on her face, even when she is trying to be serious. She especially loved his kindness and his smile.

Luke is a broker. He owns a successful chain of real estate agencies. He buys and sells high value homes and commercial properties worth millions. He is an accomplished entrepreneur, who understands business and people extremely well. He can sell anything to anyone, by knowing the client's needs and wants. He trains his agents to sell the dream, by having total confidence in their ability to close deals, and most importantly to always look the part.

Luke came to the realisation that he could not be everywhere at once. He was forced to change the way he worked, because it started taking a toll on his health. He made the decision to spend more time doing the things he loved.

He realised three years ago, he had to prioritise his health and his relationship with his family. He was spending too much time at work and not enough time creating meaningful experiences with his family. His drive to keep developing a successful business, started affecting his relationship with his wife, his daughter and physical and mental health. He was not taking the time, to do the fun things he loved.

Luke had a total reset of his life and reorganised his plans. He stopped putting an incredible amount of pressure on himself. He focused on his health, and what made him feel fulfilled and happy. He decided to work more from home and spend more time with his family. His health improved dramatically. His irrational anxiety about his business, and financial responsibilities disappeared.

He employed Wale, a young competent personal assistant, to plan his diary, organise his meetings and other commitments. After a few changes, Luke became a much happier person.

Sade enjoyed his embrace and heartbeat against her back, as they stood staring out onto the horizon.

Luke said, "Morning darling, I thought I'd make you a fresh pot of coffee after my run on the beach."

Luke smiled, as he remembered how tired she must be, working on her designs till late evening.

Luke said, "I popped my head round the studio door, last night. You were in there till late, which is why I did not want to wake you early this morning. I was hoping we could go for the run together, but you were clearly exhausted."

Sade had a busy schedule that morning. She had arranged a viewing of the completed architectural models for the new development. In appreciation of the completed project, a small celebration was planned. The whole team had worked extremely hard.

Sade said, "Luke, I am not having breakfast. It is too early for me, so I am taking mine with me. I asked Ava to make a small breakfast for you and Buki. Ava usually arrives around this time. She makes the best beans and plantain, with that delicious sauce."

Sade walked into the bedroom, as Luke went downstairs. He paused, as he past the kitchen and leaned into the entrance.

Luke said, "Morning Ava, how are you this morning."

Ava smiled and said, "Good morning ma."

Luke said, "Ava we are looking forward to your special beans, with that delicious sauce you make for breakfast. I hope there's plantain."

Ava said, "Yes, I will make beans and plantain. It will not take too long."

Ava

Ava was pleased they enjoyed her cooking. She learned how to cook as a young woman and enjoyed cooking. She mastered her dishes, and her food was delicious.

Ava works part time as a Chef, to put herself college. She wanted to further her education and own become a teacher one day. She had big plans for herself, and her family. Ava is married and has a five-year-old son. She is willing to make the sacrifices needed for her dreams to become a reality.

Ava prepared the food, before leaving to collect her son from school. Ava and her husband were from a farming community. They left their town for better opportunities in Osupa. It was a choice between, having the support of a caring family and community in their town or the opportunity to make a decent living on the island, to secure their future. Her parents still lived in the farming community. Ava visited her during the holidays, but wished she could return home more often. She spoke to her mother on the phone most evenings, to catch up on the day's events.

Ava said, "Mama, how was your day today,"

Mama Ava said, "Ava, I am so glad you called. We just finished having our dinner. I cooked your father his favourite fish dinner. He is watching the football. How is little Kayode."

Ava said, "Mama we are all well. Kayode is relaxing with their dad."

Mama Ava said, "I have some bad news about Mr Hassan down the road."

Ava took a deep breath and brassed herself for the news.

Mama Ava said, "He passed away. It was such a shock to us all. "

Ava asked what had happened to him. She remembered Mr Hassan. He was a kind man, who was always nice to Ava as a child and as a young adult. Mr Hassan would always give the smaller children a shop discount when they bought their sweets from his shop. Ava had seen children go in with toys and crayons as payment for sweets. Mr Hassan would accept pennies or crayons for a bag of sweets and give back some crayons back as change. His wife was usually nearby, keeping him company or bringing a snack into the shop. Ava never understood how he made any money. She had fond memories of him, even as a child, she knew he was a kind man.

His wife was devastated. Ava's mother noticed she had lost weight in the last few weeks. She looked a little frail. Ava's Mum and the neighbours took her cooked meals to keep an eye on her. She was terribly lonely and missed him dearly. She cried alone at night and found it difficult to sleep. Life would never be the same again without him. They had been together for more than forty years. They had two children who lived away from the village, but they did not visit that often. Ava's Mother told her about the changes that were happening at home. There was a revival in their small village. Many of the younger generation that left the village, were causing an economic revival by sending money home. Closed shops were reopening with new owners.

Ava's Mum spoke about how much she missed having Ava and her family around. It broke her heart, but she never told Ava. Having her family around her made her happy. She longed to see them again. Ava's mother spoke to her husband and prayed for them all. Her next question was always when Ava and her family were coming home for a visit.

Ava and her husband lived a modest life in the city. They faced unexpected difficulties in the city. Their life in the village was completely different, with more time for each other and their child.

In the city they both worked longer hours. When Ava was not working, she attended evening classes. She was studying to become a teacher.

Home

Luke opened the double doors at front doors of the house. He loved the carved mahogany doors. They had a carving of a wild forest, with different animals. The carved wood was creative. He liked taking his time to run his fingers across the smooth grooves of the carving. Luke thought about the craftmanship that had gone into creating such a powerful piece.

Sade commissioned the doors from one of her favourite artists. The sculptured mahogany made a powerful impression when entering the house. Luke stared at the doors for a moment, as he sipped his morning coffee.

Luke looked up at Buki coming down the stairs for breakfast.

Luke said, "Morning sleepy head, did you sleep well?"

Buki was still half asleep. Buki said, "Morning Dad yes thanks, and you?"

Luke said, "Yes dear, I slept well. Tomorrow is your big day. How are the final preparations going for the fashion show?"

Buki said, "Everything is arranged and under control. I am at home with my friend Rose today. She is coming round later for a swim later."

A few minutes later Sade came downstairs dressed for site, holding her hard hat and boots in one hand.

Buki said, "Morning Mum."

Sade said, "Morning darling, how are you feeling. You have worked extremely hard, the last couple of weeks. Your designs are so vibrant. I love the colours. Incredible, honestly. I had a look at some of your work last night. I popped into your room, but you were fast asleep."

Buki looked at her Mum with a questioning expression and a cheeky smile.

Buki said, "Thanks, Mum, but you know you are bias right? because you are my Mum. I will take the compliment though. Love you."

The theme for Buki's fashion line is Supernova, featuring an explosion of colourful designs. The show was a crucial part of her grade for her fashion design course. Her friends dressed as models with colourful wigs and makeup. All her models looked amazing. Sade and Luke were so proud and impressed with Buki's dazzling show. Sometimes Sade had to remind herself Buki was sixteen.

After the show Sade went to find Buki backstage to congratulate her, and all her amazing models on putting on a great show. Sade arranged an after party for Buki at her favourite restaurant. Her friends were there with her to celebrate with her.

The next morning Sade drove to the new construction site. She wanted to see the sculptures of the two elephants at the watering hole. She had built a waterfall, on granite steps, with water cascading into a shallow pool. The fountain was at the entrance of building. There were potted trees is huge stone vases.

When the design was completed, it created a welcoming oasis. You could hear the water gently pouring over the slate steps. The design and sculptures exceeded her client's expectations. Later that evening Luke explained he booked a property on a private estate for their vacation in Ghana. A relaxing environment was what they both needed.

Sade said, "Luke, I am glad the business is doing well. We have had consistent growth for the last couple of years with contracts coming in regularly. Remember I talked about expanding the business abroad. Well, the clients I just completed with, were so impressed with the quality of work delivered. They really liked the design, especially the stone sculptures of the elephants at the watering hole. The project I just completed was the second office space, I designed for their company. I had a final meeting with them today and they offered me a project abroad."

Luke sat on the sofa and stretched his hand out for Sade, to join him.

Sade said, "They want to fly me to London, all expenses paid. They offered to cover my accommodation and other expenses. They are going to put me up in a swanky flat, close to their newly acquired head office in Moorgate. They want to know if I can start in a couple of months. I was surprised when they asked. I have been walking on air since they asked me.

The sculptures I need can be made in the UK. If I accept the job, I could be out there for about two months, depending on the pace of the project. It is an incredible opportunity for the business. I know I usually have a team supporting me, but I was told their facilities team will be available to help."

Sade was excited. She snuggled up to Luke, with a huge smile, as he leaned in with a kiss.

Luke looked into Sade's beautiful eyes and said,

"Sade it is the opportunity, you wanted. Your determination paid off. I know you are walking on air right now; it is written all over your face. Does this mean you will be having tea at the palace."

He chuckled as he thought about afternoon tea. They stared at each other and burst out laughing at the same time. He placed his arm around her, as she moved closer to him.

Luke said, "Sade, you talked about this many times, and now it is happening. This calls for a celebration. I am cracking open that bottle I saved for a special occasion. To new beginnings!"

Sade arranged a meeting with her team the next morning. She explained she would be working remotely from London for the next two months. She had an experienced team, she trusted, and had worked with for several years. The plan was to have a remote meeting once a week to keep up to date on ongoing projects they were committed to. Her chief operations officer would oversee projects in her absence. Sade knew the transition would work well, provided she stuck to the deadline. She had three weeks to prepare for her departure.

Chapter 6

The Africa Suite London

It was summer in London. The weather was perfect, and the sun was out. Sade wore a flowing bright coloured dress, which complemented her curvaceous figure and long legs. Heathrow airport was busy, with travellers in arrivals returning from their summer holidays. Travellers wore flip flops and shorts. Hugs were exchanged with friends and families embracing at arrivals.

Sade had butterflies in her stomach, as she entered the arrivals area with her luggage. She was filled with excitement and ready for action. She brought her portfolio filled with drawings, designs, and a package of canvas paintings, wrapped in paper and plastic. The rest of the sculptures, and large ceramic terracotta pots, were arriving by air in about five days.

Sade walked through arrivals looking for her taxi. Jim had explained a driver would meet her, at the airport with her name on display. The driver would then take her to a flat, arranged for her in Angel, central London. Sade had stayed in London for short breaks before, but never like this. This was her first business trip to London. She scanned the arrivals meeting point for the driver holding up a card with her name on it. A few minutes later she noticed a tall man in a smart suit holding up her name. She smiled in his direction showing she was the person he was looking for.

Sade said, "Hello, I am Sade, you are holding up my name, you must be the driver. Thank you."

Sean said, "Hello, my name is Sean, this is my identity card. Let me take your luggage. We can take the escalator to my car; it is on the second floor of the car park. Mr McPherson asked me to call him once you arrived. I will give him a call now."

Sean said, "Hello Mr McPherson, the lady has arrived. I am handing her the phone."

Sade took the phone from Sean.

Sade said, "Hello Jim, thank you, for arranging my ride. Yes, the flight was fine. I am looking forward to taking a shower and putting my feet up."

Jim said, "you are welcome, Sade. There is food and drink when you get to the flat. Please relax and we will speak later."

Sade stared out the windows, taking in all the sights of London as they drove through the streets. Everything looked shinny and new. The roads, the cars, and the buildings. It felt as though she had brought the Sun with her.

They arrived at a contemporary, creamy coloured block of flats, set on four floors. The main entrance had an immaculate driveway with stairs leading to the main gates. The building was gated with a concierge, dressed in his smart uniform. You could see a well-kept communal garden with trees and plants beyond the entrance gates as you approached the buildings reception area.

Sean unloaded her luggage from the car and wheeled the bags into the front entrance. He asked if Sade needed anything else, to which she answered, she did not. She thanked him with a generous tip. Sade was let into the building by the concierge. He asked for her name and handed her a sealed envelope. It had a security fob and a code to access the building.

The concierge helped her, to her floor with her luggage. Sade thanked him. She tried to tip him, but he declined. He told her it was all part of the service.

She walked into the flat and was happy to see the view looked out onto the communal gardens below. The garden was a nice touch, which put a smile on her face. It reminded her of home. There were two girls lying on blankets laid out on the grass. They had a small picnic and were both reading in the warm summer sun. Sade was glad the flat had high ceilings and an open plan design. She felt comfortable, in what would be her home for the next two months.

She kicked of her shoes and walked to the Kitchen. She was pleasantly surprised to find the fridge packed with fruit juice, milk, chicken slices, cheese, fruit, vegetables, and eggs. She found fresh buns and pasta in cupboard and wondered who had done the shopping for her. There was enough food to keep her going for a few days. There were coffee beans in the cupboard and a French press. She had all she needed. She made a sandwich, which reminded her, how hungry she was, the moment she tasted it. The food tasted different, but she was too hungry to care.

Sade called Luke and Buki, once she was settled in, to let them know she had arrived safely. Her bed was calling out to her, so she kept it short. She was exhausted. She took off her clothes and curled herself under the inviting duvet. She wrapped the fresh smelling duvet round her body as she fell asleep.

Sade stayed at home for the next two days on her laptop. She contacted furniture suppliers, garden centres and upholstery suppliers. Her shipment of large, engraved terracotta standing pots, and oil paintings were arriving in a just few days.

The paintings depicted the coral reef and the surrounding ocean in Osupa. The quality was exceptional. The artist was a native of the island. He had somehow managed to capture the nature of the ocean against the backdrop of a vibrant tropical island. The use of colours in the paintings were spectacular. Sade had sourced all the other items she needed for the new layout.

She received the floor plans and pictures of the space online before she travelled. She was there to see the space physically before the furniture and other pieces arrived. Sade contacted Jim's operations director, Simone remotely. Simone had sent her the requirements for fire safety regulations, and access precautions for the spaces. The area was already painted in the colours Sade she asked. She would start working on the interior once all the furnishing and shipment arrived.

Sade had a meeting with Jim, and Simone the next morning. She presented a timeline for the completion of the works. Sade gave them delivery dates for different items. Her first invoice was approved. Sade arrived at their offices fifteen minutes before her appointment. Sade spoke to the receptionist, who informed Jim she had arrived.

Jim said, "Hi Sade, there you are, I hope you did not have problems finding the building."

Sade looked up at Jim and said,

Sade said. "Hi Jim, how are you; this must be Simone. It is a pleasure to finally meet you in person."

Simone smiled and stretched out her hand to shake Sade, as Simone looked at Sade, she thought her voice did not match the voice she had heard on the phone so often. She expected someone older, more mature. Sade was confident, charismatic, and focused on the discussion. She knew exactly what was needed and had made all the relevant arrangements. She sat down comfortably at Jim's desk and brought out her laptop.

Sade said, "Jim, can I plug my laptop into one of your monitors. That way we can all see the floor plans and drawings. I will show you the colour scheme and where the furniture, art pieces and sculptures are placed. We can then discuss the timeline and dates for deliveries. This morning I sent you both a spreadsheet with all the dates, and exactly what is being delivered and when."

Sade showed them the 3D drawings of the interior with the furniture, colours, and art pieces in place. The 3D drawings on her screen looked amazing and brought the space to life. Jim and

Simone were able to imagine what it would look like when completed. They impressed with the detail captured in the drawings.

Sade said, "I am looking forward to walking round the building to familiarise myself with the space. It looks huge without furniture. I like the space and the use of glass and light. You can see throughout the whole floor. The frosted glass is a clever way of creating separate and confidential spaces."

Sade walked around the building visualising the space with large ceramic pieces like the Osupa pots. She imagined the paintings she had bought, in the space. The large floor to ceiling glass windows meant you could see a panoramic view arial view London. The project took two months to complete. Sade worked well with Simone and Jim, who both agreed the interior met their highest expectations. Jim and Simone arranged a celebratory luncheon for Sade at the Savoy, to thank her for the interior she transformed into a stunning space.

Jim was delighted with the outcome. Sade was dynamic, and always delivered what she promised. He had been looking for the right designer to fit the new properties. He wanted Sade to inject her creativity into the project. Jim's company was an information technology company. They had offices in London, Lagos, and Atlanta.

The unique transformation Sade made on the offices made Jim realise she was someone the company needed as a partner. Jim recently bought a new office in need of refurbishment. The properties were in fashionable parts of the city. Working collaboratively with someone like Sade meant they could attract buyers willing to pay above market value for the properties.

"Sade, you have delivered the brief to the exact specification. It is tastefully done with a touch of African artistry. Once you enter this space, you do not want to leave. It is welcoming and makes you feel at ease. I especially like the tropical plants, but my favourites are the terracotta pots sculptured with ancient Yoruba designs and drawings. The designs are absolutely, gorgeous. We might need to insure them. You have transformed this space into something completely different."

The second day after completion, Jim put forward his proposal. It included free travel to the UK, as part of the terms of the new contract. Sade would be the interior designer for all their high-end UK properties. It was a big commitment and would mean several trips to the UK working on projects for short periods. Sade was flattered and excited by his proposal. It would mean collaborating closely with his team of agents. He explained the terms of the partnership. It was a little frightening, but she wanted to focus on all the positives. The rest could be worked out later.

"Jim I am really flattered. It is a big commitment and an exciting opportunity, which would mean an adjustment in the way I currently work. I would like to take some time to think about the planning and how to incorporate it into my current business model.

I hope you understand. Once I work out the planning, I will let you know. I want to thank you, for making me the offer. I will let you know my answer in the next two weeks. I need to discuss it with my team. Once I have made my decision I will be in touch."

It was not the response Jim wanted but he was willing to wait for her decision.

"Thank you, Sade, we have been looking for fresh ideas for a few years. In this industry you must evolve and reinvent your business. We need a design company with unique ideas, and your company fits the brief. More importantly we like you work ethic and commitment. I believe living on another continent, in a different environment is reflected in your designs. This is what we need right now.

We collaborate with international clients, many of whom have a home and an office in different parts of the world. They want to be impressed. You create luxurious contemporary spaces that are dynamic and impressive. Promise me, you will think about it, and let me know as soon as you can. We have several projects ready to go right now."

Sade promised she would decide in the next two weeks. The first thought that came to her mind was how she would manage all her current commitments. Her business, the support she promised the social enterprise, and her personal life.

Sade thought about Luke and Buki. She did not want the extra work to change her relationship with her family or her commitment to her company. She valued her private moments with her family and the strength of her relationship's. The morning and evening rituals at the end of each day. Those moments were invaluable. The extra responsibility would be a complete change to all their lives.

Sade could not wait to get home to have a shower. She was exhausted and needed a break from working relentlessly for the last two months. Sade wanted to relax at home, by the pool, once she had eaten her favourite, Efo Elegusi with pounded yam. She looked forward to catching up on all she had missed. Sade arrived in Osupa two days after Jim's proposal.

"Luke, I am so glad to be home. I really missed you. To be honest I did not see much of London. Temi called me to say she was in London for business with Ngozi. I met up with them twice, for drinks at a cocktail bar in Old Street close to the flat. We checked out a live band, at a bar in Wardour Street, where we danced all night long. I loved every minute of it. A welcomed break from working all the time. That was the only fun I had. Apart from that, I worked constantly. The girls had a busy schedule with wholesalers in London, which they planned, like a military operation. They arrived back a few days before me. I have to say, I was pleased with the transformation of the office space."

Sade walked around the room stripping off her hot sweaty clothes.

"The plane was freezing, but now, I am hot! The weather in London was mild but it cannot compare to 38 degrees. I am going to have a long cool shower, some food, and then, I am going to show you, just how much I missed you. Did you miss me, or did you keep yourself occupied while I was away?"

Luke looked at her, taking in all her curves and those beautiful legs. He was only half, listening to what she was saying, as she walked round their bedroom naked. He was distracted by her glow, and her curvaceous body. He fixed his gaze on her. He could not focus on what she was saying, as he stared at her body. He managed to catch the last part of what she said.

Luke said "Yes, darling off course I missed you. I tried to keep myself busy though. The boys came round a few times, it was fun. Oh, and yes! we all went out for Tom's birthday. The bar was great. The whole gang was there. I met some guys from a communications company in the US, of all places. They were in Osupa on business, determined to have fun, party hard, and that is exactly what they did."

Luke started taking his clothes off.

Luke said, "Sade, we should spend the weekend at the beach house just chilling, eating, and enjoying ourselves. No calls from the office, no emails, just relaxing. We can take lots of food and drink. We can barbeque fresh fish. It will be great. Waking up on the island is the best feeling. I feel so free down there, without a care in the world. I know you love it just as much as I do, are you game?"

Sade kissed him and walked into the shower. He moved his eyes slowly down her legs as she walked past. He started unbuttoning his shirt and trousers. He had missed touching her and waking up beside her.

Luke followed her slowly into the shower, moving his hands slowly up and down her body as the water beat down against them. Luke pulled her towards him, as he kissed her neck and moved down her body. She felt the intensity of his body against hers. She held him close as the water relaxed her muscles and all the tension in her body. Slowly the steam filled the shower until her body felt supple and easy.

A few days after her arrival, Sade got an email from Jim. He attached a new contract. He explained, she should read the contract, and return it signed if she is happy with the terms. She read it carefully. Sade knew at once, she had to get her lawyer, Lande to read the contract. She knew she would go through it with a fine-tooth comb. Lande went through all the contracts before they were signed, just in case she missed anything in the small print. Lande gave her invaluable advice. Sade referred to her work documents, as bullet proof. She adjusted the contract before Sade emailed it back to Jim and waited for the confirmation.

Sade was excited about the opportunity it created for her company. She knew consistent demand for the artwork could change her business, and the business of the artists that created it. She went home late that evening. She waited for the email from Jim. She was excited. She wanted the opportunity, even though it was a huge commitment. She got into bed and opened her laptop to find Jim's email.

Sade said, "Yes! Jim approved Lande's amendments. I was getting a bit anxious, but now it is completed, it was worth the wait."

Sade was overjoyed. Luke stood up in bed when he heard the news.

Luke said, "here is to making dreams come true. We have much to celebrate and much to be grateful for, which is why, my love, we need a party."

Luke pulled Sade out from under the sheets, he placed his right hand on her waist, and spun her round with his left. They laughed and danced to the beat of the music, blurting out of the speakers.

Chapter 7

The Visitation

Sade could hear her phone ringing. She looked at the screen. It was Yemisi.

"Hello Yemisi, how are you? This is a pleasant surprise. Is everything okay?"

Yemisi explained she needed to speak to her urgently. It was about a visit they had the day before. A small group of people had visited the island, with what looked like surveying equipment. They took pictures and asked lots of questions. They wanted to know the families that owned large estates on the island. They were interested in buying land. They spoke to a few fisher men and traders at the harbour, who told them to speak to Yemisi, if they wanted to know about land ownership on the island.

Large sections of the island were in a trust. The rest was owned by the monarchy and families on the island. They were interested in speaking to families that owned large estates on the island. They were there to gather information and make contacts. Their long-term goal was to buy and develop parts of the island. The company represented, a well-known, multinational corporation in the travel and hotel industry. They were willing to offer a great deal of money for land on the ocean front and beyond. They gave out contact details and brochures. Yemisi's family were one of the custodians of the island, like Sade's family. She wanted to know if Sade had heard of the group, because of her design construction company.

Sade had heard of them. She knew they represented a powerful and influential group. She knew they specialised in building multi story resorts for the tourist industry. She was extremely concerned because, the company was notorious, because of the way they carried-out land reclamation. They often creating irreparable damage to marine life, coral reefs, the seabed, and the ecosystem. It was impossible to predict the amount of damage they caused for years to come. The long-term financial benefits had to be measured against, long-term damage to the region.

Sade remembered watching one of the directors, bungle his way through a television interview about one of their developments. He was asked pertinent questions, about the irreparable damage the land reclamation would have on marine life, sea levels, future storms and the surrounding eco system. The interview was grilling and difficult to watch. The company had not taken reasonable care to protect the marine life in the area or consult the fishing industry. They were facing huge environmental fines.

Sade did not share this information with Yemisi. She would only worry unnecessarily. Sade simply said, she had heard of the company. Sade knew immediately, an emergency meeting of the islanders had to be called. She was friends with the prince. She would send him an urgent message asking if he was available. She wanted to know if his family were involved, or if the multinational had approached them.

Yemisi sounded worried on the phone. She was especially worried about the fishing industry in Osupa. Some of the fishing companies based on the island had contacted her earlier that day. Sade explained she would investigate the matter and get back to her.

Once the call ended, she gave Luke a concerned look. He could tell she was worried about something serious.

"It has started. They are coming for our precious Osupa."

Luke looked puzzled, and said "What has started, what are you talking about?"

Sade said, "Multinational hoteliers are trying to buy key parts of the island. They visited the island yesterday. This group builds multi storey hotels and resorts. They operate in different parts of the world. My main concern is the coral reef, and the ecological systems around the island. Everything we see now, could change forever. We need to gather the families that are thinking about selling their lands. If the area is to be developed, it must be ecologically friendly, otherwise, it goes against everything the islanders believe. The culture and traditions of the island must be respected.

It could destroy the black lipped Oysters industry. The pearl farmers are rich and influential. They have a great deal invested in Oyster farms around the island's waters. Similarly, it would have a profound impact on the fishing industry. Osupa has one of the best fishing regions, with sustainable marine life, because the ocean is left alone and allowed to develop its ecosystem."

Osupa has a unique protected system, which is kept in a sustainable way to preserve fishing and farming practices.

That evening Sade went for a long walk along the beach, with both her dogs. They were both Ridgeback dogs. They were fiercely loyal and had a majestic look about them. She loved walking with her dogs and watching them play on the beach. She felt completely relaxed and protected. The beach was quiet with only a few people strolling as the sun was setting. The dogs usually went for a run with Luke in the morning, but Sade liked taking them for a walk in the evening. Sometimes Luke joined her, or she went alone. Sade tried hard not to think about the proposed development. The dogs loved running through the shallow waves and getting their paws wet.

The sun was just setting as Sade watched the waves flowing in and out over the sand. It was a calm evening. She could see dolphins playing in the distance. Unexpectedly her dogs started barking frantically. Their barks were directed towards the end of the shoreline. She could not see what they were barking at. She noticed the strength of speed of the wind from the ocean increased. The strength of the waves was aggressive. She could feel the spray of the salty water of her face. The weather became increasingly cooler and darker. The sun had almost disappeared. The grey clouds gathering ahead, raced past the bright moon. The sudden thunder was loud enough to make her shudder.

Sade braced herself for the lightning strike. She started running towards the abandoned caves at the end of the shoreline. The lightning strike lite up the evening sky. She heard the thunder getting louder, as she reached the caves with the dogs. They were all crouched down in the cave.

Sade looked up at the sky and could tell a powerful storm was gathering. She lowered her gaze and noticed the dogs were barking at something or someone moving on the rocks in the distance. She noticed the silhouette of what looked like a sea lion and an extremely tall muscular man carrying what looked like a diving gun strapped to his back. The rocks were at the end of the shore. The man climbed down the rocks and stepped onto the sandy ground. Sade realised the silhouette of the sea lion, gradually changed into the silhouette of a woman. Once off the rocks both figures started walking slowly towards her. She noticed, as they walled their path was dry. There was no rain from above the path they walked, but everywhere else it was raining heavily. Sade quickly realised; they were approaching her. She left the cave and started walking away quicky, whilst grasping her dogs leads with both hands.

She could not understand where they had appeared from. Sade pulled her phone out of her joggers as she briskly, to ask Luke to meet her halfway home. She could not get a signal. The crashing waves, lightning strikes and thunder got louder. She could hear the winds whistling past her ears.

All she wanted to do was run home to safety. She could not understand what was happening with the freak weather. There was no warning or sign of a storm, otherwise she would have stayed home, instead of walking on the ocean front. Sade was getting increasingly anxious. She just wanted to get home as quickly as possible with her dogs.

As suddenly as the storm started, the weather calmed. The lightning and thunder stopped. It started raining gently. Sade looked up; and the grey clouds had disappeared. Sade was relieved the storm had passed and grateful she was unhurt. For a moment she thought about what might have happened. The winds had just started to pick up debris when the storm calmed.

Sade felt someone standing behind her. She turned round to see a striking bear footed woman behind her. Her hair was dry, unlike Sade's that was soaking wet from the ocean spray and rain. Her face glistened. She wore what looked like a wet body suit with a smooth soft texture. Her suit had a mother of pearl colouring, which changed as she walked in the light of the full moon.

Sade's dogs started wagging their tails, as the strangers got closer. She had not seen her dogs behave like that before. Both dogs ran up to the man and started wagging their tails in delight.

Sade tilted her head slightly and said, "This is strange. They are usually extremely cautious about strangers. I have never seen them behave like this before. They ran up to you, as though you were old friends. "

The woman stepped closer to Sade and said, "Do you remember me? The last we met you were a child. How you have changed over the years, but the sparkle in your eyes has remained. We are here to help. I can sense you have the power of prediction, am I right?"

Sade felt a spiritual connection and a deep warmth from the woman, but beneath that, she could sense a powerful intensity. Sade had not felt that type of power before. She knew instinctively she was not what she appeared to be. She felt the presence of a powerful life force.

From a young age Sade's mother had told her to keep her powers a secret, to protect herself, from those that might feel threatened by her. Sade discovered the older she got the stronger her predictions became.

She was not entirely convinced by her mother's advice. She could not understand why it was unwise to reveal her secret gift to close friends. Revealing her predictions turned out to be a grave mistake because it frightened those close to her. Sade decided to suppress her visions and sightings in response to how her predictions were received. She was forced to defend herself from bullying and abuse early on. She understood when her predictions brought an undesired outcome like sadness or loss, she became the enemy. She realised most people did not want to face the truth about the future. Today every cell in her body told her the encounter on the beach was a positive one.

Sade said, "I do not know who you are, yet I feel we have met before. Who are you and why are you both following me."

The woman said, "I bring a message from mother. You know her as the mother of oceans and rivers. We have come a long way, from another realm to give you an important message, about the impending destruction of Osupa, and the decimation of the surrounding ocean unless we change the course of events that are about to happen. This island is important. It is our first home when we arrived. This message is for you Sade, the descendant of Jibola. I know you were bestowed with the gift of prophecy from birth. You must deliver our message to the people."

The woman turned to her companion and said, "This is my brother Oshoosi. He is here because he wants justice for Osupa. He has prepared warriors to protect the island. The islanders were lied to by the multinational. They are not building a tourist resort to attract holiday makers to the island. That is a cover story. Whilst they were surveying the seabed they discovered, the ground beneath is ideal for oil drilling, a more lucrative resource. Their plan is to drill for oil, which will inevitably devastate the island and ecosystem. They intend on buying sections of the island until they own the whole island.

The island has survived many challenges over the centuries. Sade you are tasked with gathering the islanders to let them know what is happening to the island. You must use your gift. The islanders are going to need you when the time comes. We will do all we can to stop the land drilling. You must do all you can on land."

Sade instinctively knew exactly what she needed to do about the oil excavation.

Sade said, "I thought your mother was a myth, a legend. I heard the stories when I was a child, about how Jibola consulted your mother for guidance. She appeared to her in times of great crisis. Jibola dedicated her life to protecting the kingdom. I rejected my gift for many years, because of the way people reacted to my predictions.

The woman said, "You also have a gift for bringing people together to achieve something great. If you use your powers of persuasion, people will listen to you. Listening is the first step. Outsiders cannot destroy and exploit Osupa unless you and the other islanders allow them to. These are your ancestral lands, and you have the right to protect them. We will be out there, watching and supporting you every step of the way. Remember, what people do not understand they fear. You are well respected in the community. You can persuade the decision makers to change their decision if needed."

Sade said, "Thank you, I understand. What is your name."

The woman looked at Sade and smiled. She said, "I am Oya the goddess of winds storms, and lightening. We must go, the moon is rising. You should go home; it is late, and the storm has passed. You will return at the next full moon."

Sade watched as they walked away, towards the end of the coastline. Sade looked down for a moment at her dogs started barking again, when she lifted her gaze, she could see a mirage as Oya and her brother slowly disappearing. The grey clouds above cleared, and the ocean was calm. All she could hear was the sound of the waves.

Sade turned round and started running towards home. She was excited. Her heart was beating fast. She felt exhilarated and completely free for the first time in a long time. Had she really spoken to a goddess, what just happened. Her dogs ran with her all the way home, as she struggling to catch her breath.

Sade ran straight into the house and slammed the front door behind her. She grabbed Luke and hugged him as tightly as she could. Her body was trembling, and she was soaking wet. Luke hugged her closely.

Luke said, "Sade, are you all right! What happened on the beach? You look like you are in shock. You are still trembling. Sit down for a minute. I am getting you a drink. Please take a few deep breaths. Now tell me slowly, what happened."

Sade said, "I had what can only be described as an encounter on the beach. It appeared, to be a woman and a man. Remember the legend of Jibola, the visitations and sightings she and other islanders wrote about before something catastrophic was about to happen on the island. Well, I had visitation today. There were two of them. Oya and Oshoosi. They had a message Yemoja, the goddess of the ocean and rivers."

Sade was able to create a great deal of awareness. She created an event for the islanders. She spread the news quickly using all the available mediums at her disposal. The news about saving the history, the culture, and the ecosystem of Osupa went viral, on social media. Several local media stations heard about the initiative and ran the story on the local and regional news. The international news networks picked up the story about saving the island of Osupa.

Soon everyone related to the island wanted to contribute to protecting it. The sea water farmers gathered support worldwide from their customers.

Supporters came from the surrounding regions in speed boats, sailing boats, yachts, and vessels of every type to show their support for Osupa and the conservation of a much beloved island. Once those considering selling their lands found out they were deceived they cancelled all plans to sell. Sade gathered support from all those she knew in the far east, in Europe and other countries on the African continent. Sade's predictions told her, if she put the word out people would come from all over the region and beyond. There had been other paradise islands in the Atlantic that were lost to developers in the same way. Osupa had survived another attempted invasion.

Authors Note

Thank you for choosing my book.

Printed in Great Britain
by Amazon

32136475R00053